Parents and Teachers—Welcome to the M&M Fa

We strongly believe that the message found within this text will positively impact child you are enlightened by what our book has to offer.

Our goal is to create books that entertain the audience while instilling the belief that all children are responsible for contributing to society. We hope that after reading this book your child will understand that although Sam, the main character of this story, is "different"—he was born with Down syndrome, a disorder that affects one in every 750 births in America—he is still able to do what other children his age enjoy. He, like any child, is unique. In this story, Sam is celebrating his birthday by visiting a pet store and choosing a pet for his birthday gift.

Show Me Some More features:

- A main character with Down syndrome
- A chance to learn the characteristics of different animals
- Sensory and auditory stimulation through the various animals

- A lesson on thinking before making a decision
- Demonstration that disability does not set you apart from mainstream society
- Use of rhyme to entice the audience

The series of children's books we have co-authored is one of a kind. Our intention is to create a shared experience through books that are both adventurous and a learning tool for all children. Please visit the TalkTools website at WWW.TALKTOOLSTM.COM where you may contact us with any questions or comments. Additionally, you will find previews for the next books in our series that will be released in the near future. If you have not already utilized the Skill Builder or Game Kit, other components of *Show Me Some More*, you can learn more about them on the website.

Typically developed children have been exposed to inclusion but do not fully understand its true meaning. Inside the back cover of this book, teachers can find ideas on how to generate a discussion within the classroom concerning inclusion of children with Down syndrome as well as those with other "special needs."

Continue to give children a special gift, and read to them each day!

Sincerely,

Michael F. Cianciulli and Michael T. Cianciulli

TALK TOOLS®
INNOVATIVE THERAPISTS INTERNATIONAL

WWW.TALKTOOLSTM.COM

4/28/05

Paul Brady -

Continue to read
each day!

Best Wishes

Michael Chanculli

Michael Chanculli

SHOW ME SOME MORE

To Cayman

Our family pet who has brought much
joy and love to our household

M&M Cianciulli

Time to go

Let's pack the van
We're off today
That's the plan.

Molly held his hand
As Sam led the way
The family was off
To celebrate Sam's birthday!

Clicking and snapping
Was heard from inside
Seatbelts were buckled
And locked for the ride.

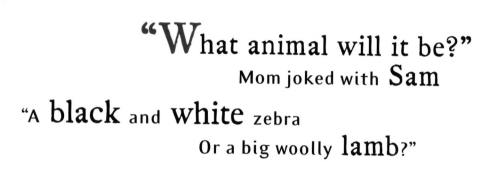

"What animal will it be?"
Mom joked with Sam

"A black and white zebra
Or a big woolly lamb?"

Fluffy or furry
But not really wet
Young little Sam

Wanted a pet . . .

"Sure honey, whatever
The choice is up to you
It's your **birthday** gift
We hope to like it too."

The van slowly rolled
Into the small lot
"Mom, is it all right
If I name my pet SP**O**T?"

"What will it be?"

said the man at the store
"Gosh, we don't know
We're barely in the door."

"We like what we see
Do you have any more?
We're not sure which pet
Sam is looking for."

"While you are here
Please have some tea
No need to worry
It's all for f r e e ! "

Each part of the store
Was filled with pets
Some that little Sam
Hadn't heard of yet.

They
BARKED
meeeoooooooooowed

HISSSSSSSSSED
and purrrrred

Some even
TWEETED
Like the big ol' bird.

"Come with me
I'll show you each one
You can touch and feel
And choose when we're done."

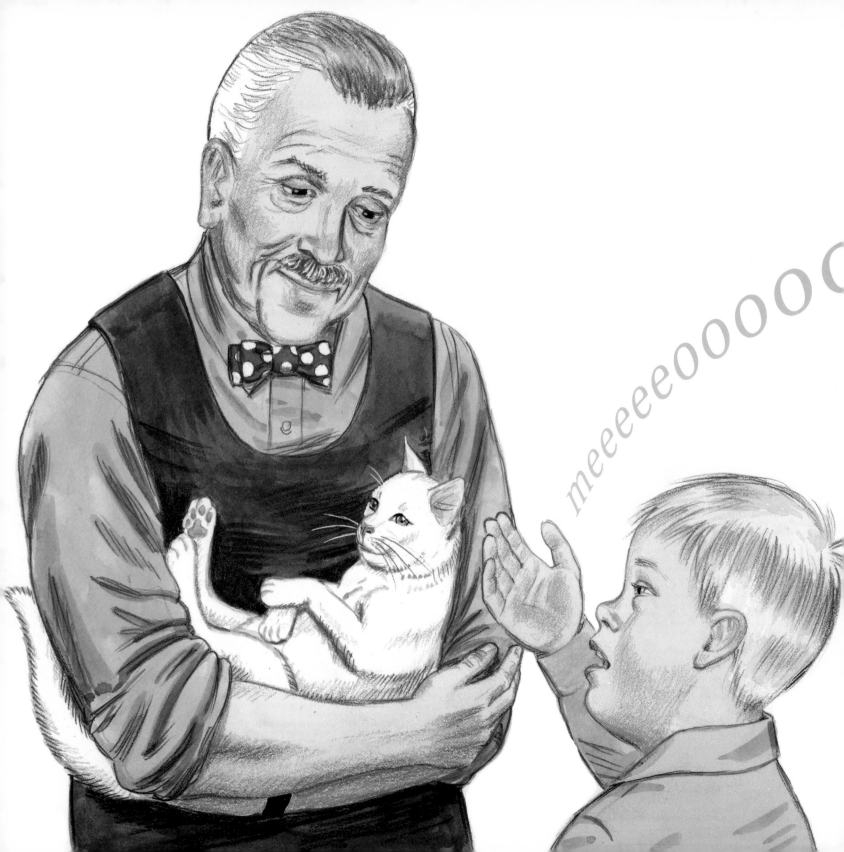

meeeeeooooo

booow

Frank chose a white kitty
Fluffy with fur
She jumped and played
And started to purr.

"You can make the sound
Of each animal we see
Go ahead and try it
How happy they'll be."

"What do you think?"
Said the man at the store

"Gosh, I don't know
Show me some more."

"Look at these tanks
Filled with tropical fish
Darting in and out
Which do you wish?

"The colors are bright
Red, orange and yellow
Boy they swim *fast*
My little fellow."

"What do you think?"
Said the man at the store

"Gosh, I don't know
Show me some more."

On to the next— "Look it's a snake He is one of my friends We call him Jake. He's long and he's quiet And he likes to sssssssssssssssssssssssssssslither By golly, I hope he doesn't make you quiver."

"Feel how cold
His body can be
When he's outdoors
He'd be in a tree."

"What do you think?"
Said the man at the store

"Gosh, I don't know
Show me some more."

"Quick, over here!
Look at this **tail**
It's fluffy and white
And always for **sale**."

"Some bunnies are tan
While others are **brown**
Oh, did I mention
They **hop** up and **down**?"

"The small bunny's fur
Is **soft** to **stroke**
Go ahead, be **friendly**
Give it a **poke**."

"What do you think?"
Said the man at the **store**

"Gosh, I don't know
Show me some more."

"This animal is green
With a very hard shell
   Any idea what it is?"
Sam couldn't tell.

   "It's a turtle!" Frank said
Picking it up
   He caught Sam staring
At a cute little pup.

   "A turtle is slow
But can swim and walk
   And he'll always listen
If you want to talk."

   "What do you think?"
   Said the man at the store

   "Gosh, I don't know
      Show me some more."

"I saw you looking
At that crate over **there**
What is that animal
All covered with **hair?**"

"It's a small **puppy!**"

Sam said with a **smile**
"He's **wagging** his tail
Been **BARKING** awhile."

"He's so happy to see you
He will gladly **obey**
Take the ball over
So you two can **play**."

"Toss the ball out
He loves to fetch
    With a little more practice
He'll be ready to catch."

"What do you think?"
Said the man at the store
"Made my decision
I don't need to see more."

The turtle was cute
His shell **hard** and **all**
But Sam really wants
A **pet** that gets **tall**.

Jake the snake
Doesn't **grow** in **height**
How would Sam walk him?
That doesn't seem right.

It must be furry
That's the right **feel**
In a moment Sam's choice
He will reveal.

The kitty and bunny
Were also great
But Sam chose the
Puppy to be his mate.

As the puppy and Sam
Met to embrace
A smile could be seen
On everyone's face!

Sam's new puppy!

Please color this sticker
And when you are done
Add it to your Talk Tools Tool Box™
For extra fun!